A Gift For:

_____

From:

_____

How to Use Your Interactive Story Buddy®:

1. Activate your Story Buddy by pressing the "On / Off" button on the ear.
2. Read the story aloud in a quiet place. Speak in a clear voice when you see the highlighted phrases.
3. Listen to your Story Buddy respond with several different phrases throughout the book.

Clarity and speed of reading affect the way Bell®responds. She may not always respond to young children.

Watch for even more Interactive Story Buddy characters. For more information, visit us on the Web at Hallmark.com/StoryBuddy.

 I Reply TECHNOLOGY®

Hallmark's **1 Reply Technology** brings your Story Buddy® to life! When you read the key phrases out loud, your Story Buddy gives a variety of responses, so each time you read feels as magical as the first.

Copyright © 2013 Hallmark Licensing, LLC

Published by Hallmark Gift Books, a division of Hallmark Cards, Inc., Kansas City, MO 64141
Visit us on the Web at Hallmark.com

All rights reserved. No part of this publication may be reproduced, transmitted, or stored in any form or by any means without the prior written permission of the publisher.

Editorial Director: Carrie Bolin
Editor: Emily Osborn
Art Director: Chris Opheim

Designer: Mary Eakin
Production Designer: Dan Horton
Photographers: Jake Johnson, Steve Wilson
Photo Stylists: Landon Collis, Betsy Gantt
Photo Retouchers: Tim Bishop, Greg Ham, Thomas Ginther, Theresa Medford, Bert Hicks
CGI/Multimedia Designers: Ira Baker, Paul Horton, Michael Shockey, Steve Goslin
Project Coordinators: Kim Muir, Jennifer Fisher

ISBN: 978-1-59530-608-1
KOB1078

Printed and bound in China
JUN13

BOOK 2

Bell's Blue Ribbon

By Tom Shay-Zapien

There are lots of big events in Pineville, but the one Bell was most excited about was the Pineville Pet Show.

Bell thought of winning the Prettiest Puppy ribbon with Sofia right beside her, and that made Bell smile.

Bell had won lots of ribbons in Palm City pet shows, but not without a little bit of practice . . . and pampering.

Since she already knew all her tricks, she and Sofia stopped by the Pineville Pet Store before the big day. "C'mon, Bell!" smiled Sofia. "It's time to get beautiful!"

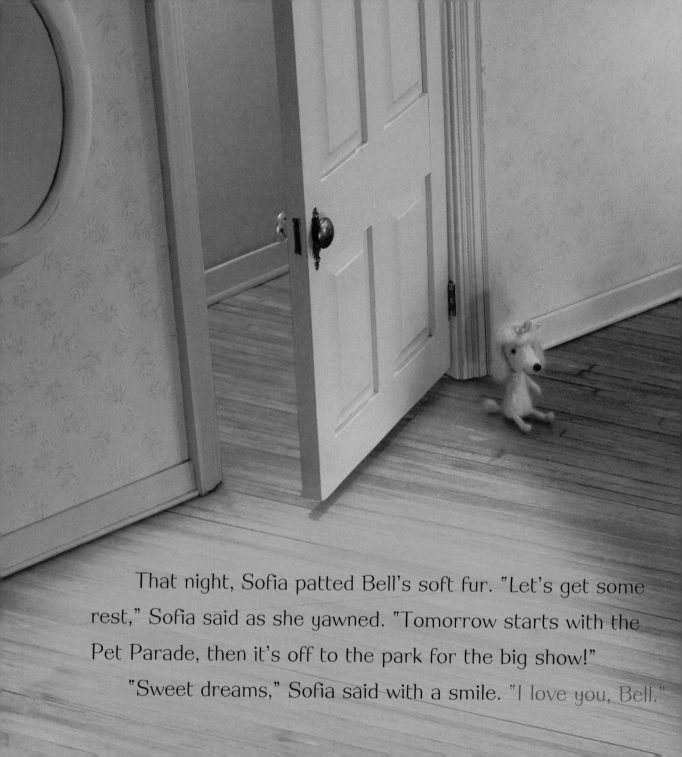

That night, Sofia patted Bell's soft fur. "Let's get some rest," Sofia said as she yawned. "Tomorrow starts with the Pet Parade, then it's off to the park for the big show!"

"Sweet dreams," Sofia said with a smile. "I love you, Bell."

Excitement filled the air as pets and their owners lined up along Main Street. Sofia waved to Andrew and Jingle and several of her Pineville friends.

Bell and Sofia had never been in a parade before, and so far,
it was better than they dreamed it would be.

"Look at all these people!" beamed Sofia. "Are you ready for
a fun time?"

Families and friends lined the street as Sofia and Bell led the way. Several people along the parade route complimented Bell as she pranced proudly beside her friends.

"What a charming dog!" said Mrs. Carlson.

Sofia smiled. "Bell, can you say *thank you?*"

Before the judging started, Andrew and Jingle stopped by to wish Sofia and Bell good luck. Bell was busy practicing her new trick.

"Whoa!" shouted Andrew. "That's really cool! Bell, you're such a pretty puppy!"

As the contestants took their positions, the judges made their way onto the field. Bell sat very still as Sofia tended to some last-minute grooming.

"Okay, Bell," said Sofia. "It's almost our turn. Are you ready for a fun time?"

Just as Bell was about to do her trick for the judges, there was a loud crash. Everyone turned toward Kevin. His hamster ball had fallen to the ground with his hamster, Truman, still inside.

Kevin clumsily chased after the hamster ball, but it was going too fast! Truman was quickly headed toward a big hill that ended at a busy street! Instinctively, Bell ran after the ball. She jumped to try and catch it, but instead fell into a big puddle.

"C'mon, guys!" Sofia called out to her friends. "It looks like Bell could use a little help!"

Bell shook herself off and kept running. Just as the ball was about to roll down the hill, Bell jumped in front of the ball and stopped it with her paw.

The kids caught up as Bell nudged the hamster ball toward Kevin. "Truman!" Kevin shouted. "Bell! You saved Truman!"

"Oh, Bell," said Sofia, as she hugged her soaked husky pup. "Are you OK?" Although she was happy to have helped, being wet did not make Bell very happy.

Sofia did everything she could think of to get Bell ready for the judges, but there was just no hiding the fact that she looked nothing like she did when she arrived that morning.

Sofia tried her best to smile as she prepared for the big trick. Bell's tail wagged as Sofia reached into her pocket. "Bell, do you want a treat?"

The crowd applauded as Bell jumped, twirled, and caught the treat in midair. After that, the judges moved on to look at the remaining pets.

Sofia knelt beside Bell and spoke softly into her ear. "Ribbon or no ribbon, you'll always be my very best friend. I love you, Bell."

After all the ribbons had been passed out, and Sofia realized there wouldn't be a Prettiest Puppy award to add to Bell's collection, a tiny tear ran down her cheek. That's when the main judge asked for everyone's attention so he could make a special announcement.

"This year we have a special award to give out—the Blue Ribbon of Bravery," said the judge. "Congratulations, Bell!"

The crowd cheered. Sofia clapped. "Oh, Bell, can you say *thank you?*"

As the Pineville Press snapped a photo of all the contestants,
Sofia snuggled closely to her heroic little husky pup.

"We sure are lucky," Sofia whispered to Bell.
"We have so many friends. And there's nothing
better than a good friend."

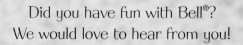

Did you have fun with Bell®?
We would love to hear from you!

Please send your comments to:

Hallmark Book Feedback

P.O. Box 419034

Mail Drop 215

Kansas City, MO 64141

Or e-mail us at:

booknotes@hallmark.com